Pearl Harbor Is Burning!

About the ONCE UPON AMERICA® Series

Who is affected by the events of history? Not only the famous and powerful. Individuals from every part of society contribute a *story*—and so weave together *history*. Some of the finest storytellers bring their talents to this series of historical fiction, based on careful research and designed specifically for readers ages 7–11. These are tales of young people growing up in a young, dynamic country. Each ONCE UPON AMERICA® volume shapes the reader's understanding of the people who built America and of his or her own role in our unfolding history. For history is a story that we continue to write, with a chapter for each of us beginning "Once upon America."

Pearl Harbor Is Burning!

A STORY OF WORLD WAR II

BY KATHLEEN V. KUDLINSKI
ILLUSTRATED BY RONALD HIMLER

PUFFIN BOOKS

Many thanks to Sensei H. Tadao Imoto,
Goju-Ryu Karate-do

PUFFIN BOOKS
Published by the Penguin Group
Penguin Books USA Inc., 375 Hudson Street, New York, New York 10014, U.S.A.
Penguin Books Ltd, 27 Wrights Lane, London W8 5TZ, England
Penguin Books Australia Ltd, Ringwood, Victoria, Australia
Penguin Books Canada Ltd, 10 Alcorn Avenue, Toronto, Ontario, Canada M4V 3B2
Penguin Books (N.Z.) Ltd, 182–190 Wairau Road, Auckland 10, New Zealand

Penguin Books Ltd, Registered Offices: Harmondsworth, Middlesex, England

First published in the United States of America by Viking Penguin,
a division of Penguin Books USA Inc., 1991
Published in Puffin Books, 1993

1   3   5   7   9   10   8   6   4   2

LIBRARY OF CONGRESS CATALOGING-IN-PUBLICATION DATA
Kudlinski, Kathleen V.
Pearl Harbor is burning!: a story of World War II / by Kathleen
V. Kudlinski; illustrated by Ronald Himler.
p.   cm.—(Once upon America)
"First published in the United States of America by Viking
Penguin, a division of Penguin Books USA Inc., 1991"—T.p. verso.
Summary: When his family moves to Hawaii in 1941, Frank feels out
of place until he makes friends with a Japanese American boy—the
day before the bombing of Pearl Harbor.
ISBN 0-14-034509-4
1. Pearl Harbor (Hawaii), Attack on, 1941—Juvenile fiction.
[1. Pearl Harbor (Hawaii), Attack on, 1941—Fiction.   2. World War,
1939–1945—Fiction.   3. Japanese Americans—Fiction.   4. Hawaii—
Fiction.]   I. Himler, Ronald, ill.   II. Title.   III. Series.
[PZ7.K9486PE 1993]   [Fic]—dc20   93-15135   CIP   AC
Printed in the United States of America

ONCE UPON AMERICA® is a registered trademark of Viking Penguin,
a division of Penguin Books USA Inc.

To Deborah Brodie,
gifted editor, valued friend

Contents

Aloha, Dummy

"Hey, you dumb *haoli,* you stop!"

Frank wanted to look back, to yell at the boy who was following him up the hill. But he knew better than to stop.

Why won't they leave me alone? Frank wondered. Dad had said that Hawaii was a friendly place. It wasn't that way for a fifth grade boy. Especially not a *haoli* from the mainland.

"Hey, *how-lee!*" The boy was by his elbow now. "You no can hear?"

Frank kept climbing the hill. He thought the boy was in his class at school, but he wasn't sure. He'd never been around so many Asians. It wasn't this way in Maryland. Two more island boys caught up with them. One bumped into Frank's shoulder.

"You all leave me alone." Frank tried not to sound scared. He hurried across the road behind a pineapple truck. The boys followed. Frank walked faster, his leather shoes slipping in the sandy dirt. Why wouldn't his mother let him go barefoot like everybody else here?

They were almost running. One of the boys knocked against his arm. Frank twisted, trying to catch his books, but they slipped out of his hand and tumbled down the hill behind him. He stopped and glared at the boys.

"*Aloha, haoli!*" one of them said, with a mean grin. Frank took a step back and ran into another boy.

"Ow!" one of them cried.

When Frank leaned over to see what had happened, somebody shoved him from behind and yelled, "Have a nice trip, dummy!" Frank fell in a crazy sort of somersault onto the road.

He could hear the boys laughing as he scrambled off the road. Another pineapple truck blew its horn. The boys ran into the bushes or on up the street.

2

The truck roared by a few feet from Frank's face, spraying sandy red dirt into his eyes.

The stink of gas and pineapple on the dusty roadside made him want to choke. Sand burned in his eyes. *Don't rub them,* he kept telling himself. Instead he rubbed his knees. The shredded fabric of his pants was sticky with dirt and fresh blood.

"Hey, *haoli!*"

Frank shook his head and squinted into the tropical sun. Another boy walked over to him and held out his hand. Frank wiped tears off his cheeks, and with them, the last of the sand. This boy looked Asian, too.

Frank looked back up the sidewalk to see the gang running away. "You one of them?" Frank asked.

The boy shook his head, no. "I am Kenji. You need help to get books?" Frank reached for Kenji's hand and got to his feet. He groaned as his pants legs moved over his raw skin.

He looked straight at Kenji. "Hey, wait. You're in my class. Isn't your name George?"

The boy gave him a friendly grin. "That my English name. My school name. Everywhere else, I am Kenji."

"Does everyone have two names here?" Kenji nodded. That was why he hadn't been able to figure out who was in his class, Frank thought.

The boys began gathering the scattered schoolwork. It took a while. They found Frank's math paper in a flower bush. His reading book was on somebody's lawn. His spelling work had fresh tire tracks across the back.

"Those creeps could have killed me," he grumbled when he found his library book. Its cover, with the picture of Babe Ruth on it, was almost ripped off.

"No. They just fooling around. Bullies. They give every new *haoli* a hard time for a while." Kenji handed Frank his arithmetic book. "Those guys study judo with me. If they wanted to, they would hurt you bad."

Frank wanted to ask what judo was. There certainly wasn't any of it in Maryland. But he didn't want to look stupid. Instead, he asked, "What kind of a name is Kenji?" as they gathered up the last of his books.

"Japanese."

"Swell! I've never known anybody from Japan."

"You dumb *haoli*. I was born in Hawaii. Me one American like you."

"Oh." Kenji didn't look or sound like any American Frank had ever known, but it wouldn't be polite to say so. "Well, uh, thanks for the help."

Frank grunted as the pile of books bumped into his sore ribs. He shifted them into his other arm, and began limping back up the hill. To his surprise, Kenji came along.

"You like baseball?" Kenji asked, pointing to the tattered library book Frank held.

"I pitch."

"You any good?"

Frank nodded. "Our team was 12 and 0 last spring. Does Pearl City School have a team?"

"We were tops in 1941, too! Our best pitcher just moved off island. We sure can use you!"

That sounded great, Frank thought. Maybe Kenji could introduce him to some other team members. Ones he could really be friends with. For now at least he had somebody to talk to.

"You collect baseball cards?" he asked. When Kenji nodded, Frank grinned. "Do you trade? I have an extra 1937 Joe DiMaggio. Maybe we could throw a ball around, too." Frank stopped by the gate to his house. "Hey, you didn't have to walk me home."

"I live two doors down the street from you. My father owns your house."

Now Frank did feel dumb. "How come I never see you on the street?" he asked in surprise.

"I don't have much time. After school, I take classes in Japanese. Saturdays, I go to classes at the Japanese Community Center at the Buddhist temple."

"What about Sunday? I've got a tree fort down

in the gully by Pearl Harbor. Want to play there in the morning?"

"*You* built that? I've seen it on my way home from the Center. It's swell!"

"We'd have to get there early," Frank said. "I have to be home and cleaned up in time for church."

"Is six too early?" Kenji asked. Frank shook his head, no. "Great. Don't forget your baseball cards!" Kenji waved and headed down the street.

Kenji could find me a friend, Frank thought. *After a month in Hawaii, I finally might meet a friend here.* He took a deep breath. "I *do* have friends," he said out loud. "Lots of them." Then, more quietly, "But they're all 10,000 miles away."

Frank walked slowly up the front steps. His mother wouldn't like Kenji at all. He knew what she'd say. "He's not the sort of boy your father and I want you to spend time with." Frank decided that he just wouldn't tell her about Kenji.

"Hurry, Franklin." She met him at the door. "I've finally found a nice friend for you. He's waiting inside." She looked out over his head. "And just who was that walking with you?"

Island Boy

"I'm waiting, young man." Frank's mother stood in the hallway, her hands on her hips. "Who was that boy?"

"His name is Kenji. He says his father owns this house."

"Oh. Yes." Mrs. Hopkins paused. "Well, do come in and meet Weston." She glanced down at his ripped pants. "Do I need to look at those knees?" Frank shook his head. Having a hospital nurse for a mother was great. When he really needed help, she knew just what to do. And she'd seen so much in the emergency room back home that she never got upset over little scrapes. "Go and change, then," she said. "Hurry now, you hear?"

Frank ran cold water on a washcloth and washed off the dried blood. When he looked into the mirror, he scowled. His normally blue eyes were red from the sand. Would Weston think he'd been crying? He splashed his face with cold water. More reddish dirt fell out of his hair. He hurried into a fresh pair of pants and joined his mother in the living room.

"Frank," his mother said, "this is Mrs. Griffith and Weston."

"I'm pleased to meet you, ma'am," Frank said, shaking her hand. He knew he would be scolded later if he forgot his manners. He turned to look into a pair of the palest blue eyes he had ever seen. "Pleased to meet you," he said to Weston. Frank could almost hear his mother smile.

"Why don't you boys help yourselves to a brownie and go out to play?" she suggested.

Frank led the way to the kitchen and poured two cups of milk. Weston helped himself to a brownie from a plate on the kitchen table, and asked, "Why are you living in Hawaii?"

"My father is a newspaper editor. He's here to work on the *Honolulu Star Bulletin.* He said we'd get to know the real Hawaii if we came for a year instead of just for a vacation."

"My father is a Navy doctor," Weston said, "so we get to live on the base with all the other Navy families. I go to school there." He had another brownie. "Are there real Hawaiians at your school?"

"Sure. And real Chinese." Frank grabbed a second brownie, too. "And real Japanese. And real Filipinos. And even a couple of other *haolis*."

"What's a *haoli?*"

"That's you and me. White kids from the mainland." Frank's knees were stinging. "They're not very friendly to *haolis* here."

"You should be on a military base. Most everybody is new, so everybody is friendly. And you don't have to mix with the locals."

Frank decided to ask his dad if they could move to the base, too.

"Did you leave us some brownies?" Mrs. Hopkins called from the living room. The boys quickly looked down at the plate. There were two pieces left. They grinned at each other and carried the plate in to serve their mothers.

"And, Margaret, you should see the strange foods they eat," Frank's mother was complaining. "It's almost impossible to make a proper meal here. And all these odd fruits!" Frank's mother threw up her hands.

Mrs. Griffith shook her head. "You should come shopping on the base with me. It's just like a store back home."

"Oh, could I? I miss the States so." Mrs. Hopkins seemed to remember the boys. "Why don't you two play outside now?" She turned to Weston's mother. "Frank hasn't found a single friend on his own here."

"I do too have a friend," Frank said quickly. "His name is Kenji. We're getting together Sunday morning."

"You told that boy you'd meet him?" Mrs. Hopkins's voice was cool. When Frank nodded, she said, "Well, Franklin, of course you must follow through with your promise and see him this once."

As soon as they were outside, Frank took a deep breath. The warm ocean breeze smelled good after the stuffy air in the living room. Most people in Hawaii, he had noticed, sat on their porches to enjoy the soft wind. They even ate supper in the shade of the porch roof. The Hopkins family had never tried that.

Frank picked up his mitt and tossed a ball to Weston. He missed it. "You need to warm up a bit?" Frank asked.

"No. I don't play baseball."

"You don't?" Frank was stunned. "What do you play?"

"I play chess. Do you?"

12

Frank shook his head. What was there to talk about? "I have a tree fort down in the gully. Want to see it?"

This time, Weston shook his head, no. "Too many bugs in those places. I guess we'll have to play ball."

No matter how easy Frank made his throws to Weston, his new friend couldn't catch them. "You want to practice your pitching instead?" Frank offered. Weston shrugged. "See the old tire under that tree? Try to throw the ball through it, like this."

Frank wound up and pitched the ball cleanly through the tire. He pointed to the mark by his toe. "From here to that tire is exactly how far it is from a pitcher's mound to home plate. I even hung the tire at just the right height for a fair pitch." Weston's face looked blank. "Just try it," Frank finally said.

Weston's first pitch flew over the tire. The next one was wide. Weston threw five more balls without sending one through the tire.

"I said chess is my game," he said stiffly.

Frank could feel how upset Weston was. "I've never even tried chess," he offered. "Could you teach me some this afternoon?"

"I don't play much with beginners anymore."

"Boys!" Frank's mother called from the back door. "You all come in, now."

They walked silently to the door. "I've asked

Weston and his mother to come back on Monday. Won't that be nice?"

Frank's father came home just as the guests were leaving. "I've heard a lot about your husband, Mrs. Griffith," he said. Weston grinned. Frank tried not to put weight on his sore knees.

It seemed forever before the Griffiths left. Finally Mrs. Hopkins started dinner and Frank and his father could go out to the backyard.

"Young Weston seems a bit stiff," Frank's father said, as they took turns pitching through the tire.

Frank grinned. "He doesn't like baseball, Dad. He isn't interested in my tree house. And he's scared of pineapple bugs." The balls sailed through the tire with a steady rhythm.

"There's nothing for Weston and me to talk about. And now I have to spend all Monday with him, too."

"Sometimes the best kind of friends are the ones who teach us new things."

"He won't," Frank said sharply.

"Won't what?"

"He said he wouldn't teach me chess."

"*I* can do that," Mr. Hopkins said. Frank looked at him in surprise. His father laughed and nodded. "It's been a long time since I played, but I still remember enough to teach you."

As they gathered the balls under the tree, Frank

imagined how Weston's face would look if he beat him at chess on Monday. He looked up at the shiny red mountain apples. The other boys ate them. He picked one and took a bite. A starchy sweet taste filled his mouth.

Everything was perfect. The evening sun was warm, his arm muscles felt good from pitching just right, and his father was home. Hawaii wasn't so bad, after all.

"Frank," Mr. Hopkins said. "Are you sure that fruit is safe?"

"It no can hurt you," Frank said. His father laughed loud and long before Frank realized what he had said. He blushed. "I mean it can't hurt you."

"My island boy." Mr. Griffith put his arm around Frank and walked him into the house. "Martha, your boy is eating island fruit and speaking Pidgin English already. He'll be a native before we know it."

"Not in my house," she said sharply. "Now, wash up for dinner."

Attack!

Frank was panting by the time he reached his tree fort. He unzipped his Baltimore Orioles jacket. It would never be this warm at home on December 7, he thought. "Kenji?" he called. "You here yet?"

"Eyes up!" Kenji yelled from above his head. "Pop fly headed for center field!" Frank saw only a flash as Kenji tossed a ball at him from the fort.

Without thinking, Frank cupped his hands. He found the ball against the silvery banyan leaves, and caught it easily.

He threw it back at Kenji. "You're out!" he yelled.

"Swell catch!" Kenji grinned at him over the driftwood railing. "Hey, I wait half-hour for you. I thought you no come, it got so late."

"My mom didn't make it easy," Frank said. "Oops—she no make it easy," he corrected himself.

"Hey, *haoli*, you no have to talk Pidgin with me. I know English from school. Besides, all kids talk Pidgin when they stay in Hawaii. You don't have to try. It just happen."

"Where does Pidgin English come from?" Frank asked. It wasn't anything he'd ever heard about before he came to Hawaii.

"All kind of kids from all over the world come to islands. Or maybe all kind of men. Nobody talk the same, but they want to be friends." Kenji moved over to make room as Frank climbed up onto the tree-house floor beside him. "So they make their own way of talking, with words from all their homes. Hey, this is some fort!"

Frank looked around with pride. The tree house sagged on one side, but it was lashed tight with rope he'd found on the beach. Tides had brought him every piece of driftwood he had used, too, and every old crate and colorful fishing float. He had gathered it, day by day. Then he carried it all up the hill through soggy, shoulder-high ferns. Finally, he had pulled each piece up into the tree and lashed it into place.

"But *that's* the best part," Frank said, waving at the view over Pearl Harbor. "The whole Pacific fleet is here. Dad said there are more than 90 Navy ships in the harbor right now."

He put his hand in a pocket. "Say, I brought some ham biscuits for breakfast. Want one?"

Kenji reached into his own pocket. "I bring something for you, too," he said with a grin. "You ever try rice balls?"

The boys traded, and Frank saw that Kenji was watching him closely. "Thanks," he said and bit deeply into the fist-sized ball of rice. His face puckered as the rice ball fell apart in his mouth. Something horribly sour and salty was hidden in the ball. He'd been tricked!

Frank wanted to spit it out, but Kenji was still grinning, so he chewed, instead. The flavors melted together and the taste changed. It was a little sweet, too, Frank realized. He swallowed hard, and made himself smile back at Kenji. Why hadn't he brought a canteen of water with him? He stuffed the other half of the rice ball in his mouth.

Without the surprise this time, Frank enjoyed the strong sharp flavor hidden inside the rice. It was still a strange taste, but good.

"You like?" Kenji asked. "I've got more." They shared the rest of their breakfasts, looking out over the harbor.

The rising sun gleamed on the smokestacks of huge battleships tied to concrete pilings off Ford Island. It looked like a whole city of war, its skyscrapers bristling with guns and gangways, flags and conning towers.

"The farthest one from here is the *Maryland*," Frank pointed out proudly. "That's where I live. Or lived. Well, Maryland is where I'm going back to next year." They looked out at the battleship together. "Dad got me a map of the ships so I could pick her out. Those over there are destroyers. The little ones are cruisers."

"Little?" Kenji asked, and they both laughed. The cruisers were enormous, even at this distance.

"Hey, did you bring your baseball cards?"

Kenji grinned. "Of course." As they dug into their pockets, a buzzing sound filled the sky. Kenji didn't even look up. "There they are again. Practice raids. Sometimes all the planes make my mother's head hurt."

Frank suddenly wondered about Kenji's family. What was a Japanese mother like? A Japanese-American mother, he corrected himself. Would she wear a kimono or a housedress? Did Kenji's father ever pitch balls?

20

A deep thumping sound reached them across the water, and both boys turned to see a dark plane heading right for them. As it pulled up to clear the hillside, they could see a bright red ball painted on its side.

"It's a Japanese plane!" Kenji screamed into the roar of its engines.

"They're bombing Hickham Field!" Frank shouted. Both boys stood to get a view of the far airstrip. Giant black clouds bloomed, blew away with the wind, and bloomed again. The low thumping of each explosion rolled slowly across the water. Flames soared over the Army aircraft parked on the ground.

Japanese planes swooped overhead from every direction. Frank had never seen so many planes in the sky at once. It was beautiful. Exciting. Loud. But it couldn't be real. It looked like the Fourth of July and an old war movie all rolled together. While he held his ears against the roar, Frank saw a plane drop a bomb into the water.

Bombing the water? he wondered. Then he realized what he'd seen. "A torpedo!" he cried.

A cruiser exploded into a red burst of flame. Now oily black smoke was billowing all around Pearl Harbor. Air raid sirens began to scream from every ship.

"Here come some more!" yelled Kenji. These planes were flying so low that the wind from their

propellers whipped the water into whitecaps. And they were heading straight toward the battleships. The boys saw them drop torpedo after torpedo, before they pulled up at the last minute to roar away into the sky.

"That's the *Oklahoma!*" Frank shouted as the first big battleship took a hit. "There goes the *West Virginia!*"

"Jeez! Look at that one!" Kenji cried over the thundering drone of hundreds of airplanes.

"That's the *Arizona!*" Frank yelled, watching the ship burst into flame. "And they got it again!" Oil slicks flooding across the water were on fire.

"No! No!" Frank and Kenji shrieked. They stamped their feet as another battleship took a double hit. They had to grab a branch as some of Frank's carefully tied knots slipped. "That was the *California!*" he shouted.

"It almost got *us*, too!" Kenji laughed nervously as the tree fort settled to a sharper tilt. "Oh, look!"

A Japanese plane tumbled into the harbor below the fort. "Hooray!" Both boys recklessly stamped their feet again.

Now anti-aircraft fire began exploding in puffs of black smoke. "Get him! Get him!" They cheered the U.S. Navy on.

An explosion tore apart the corner of the nearest destroyer. For the first time, the boys could see tiny figures running to and fro on the burning ship. "The *Nevada*," Frank said, but the glee had gone out of his voice.

Choking smoke blew past the boys, bringing with it the faint sound of men screaming. They watched in horror as the giant *West Virginia* slowly sank to the shallow bottom of the harbor, sending waves crashing against the beach below them.

Two more bombs exploded on the *Arizona*. Then the *Oklahoma* started to roll. The whole ship slowly turned over and settled into the mud. It was too real now. Frank didn't want to see any more, but he couldn't look away.

The harbor was full of sirens and smoke and men scrambling for safety. Suddenly a blinding light flashed across the water. The *Arizona* exploded in a huge ball of flame that filled the sky and sent shock waves to sweep men off the decks of all the nearby ships. When the sound hit Frank, he thought his ears would burst. There couldn't be anything left of that ship, he thought.

And still the planes kept coming. Bombs dropped until the air was one steady sound of explosion, drowning out the roar of the planes.

When the attack ended, the boys stood silently. Finally, Frank wiped his eyes and began picking up the scattered baseball cards. His ears still rang. His mind was numb. He glanced at his watch. The

whole attack had taken less than half an hour!

Out in the harbor, ship engines began rumbling. Some raced to help other ships or to rescue men from the burning waters. A few headed out to sea. The huge *Nevada* slowly pulled away from Ford Island, heading for the open ocean, her gun barrels pointed skyward.

"Oh, no!" Frank moaned, as the sky filled again. The Japanese were back with a second attack. It wasn't fair! But this time, Frank and Kenji cheered. Now the U.S. Navy was fighting back. Shells streaked upward from every ship that could fire at the planes. Even those ships pulled up out of the water for repairs were fighting this attack.

More destroyers and cruisers were hit; more were sunk. Finally, with one last shattering explosion, the sky was clear again.

"Will they be back?" Kenji wondered over the sounds of sirens.

"I don't know," Frank answered, looking at the smoke-filled harbor. "But we have to do something to help!"

The Race

"You go to help, Frank. I go home."

Frank looked at Kenji. "You've got to be kidding! What are you—scared?"

"A son's first duty is to his family." The way Kenji said it made Frank think of the Ten Commandments. It also made him think of his own mother. She would be worried.

"Oh . . ." He started to argue, but Kenji was already climbing down the rope ladder. Frank looked back at the smoke-filled harbor. Sirens wailed from every direction. "Wait up, Kenji!" he called.

They scrambled through the ferns and vines to-gether. A police car roared past, sending a cloud of powdery white sand into their faces. Another police car followed, siren blasting, and then another.

"Come on, let's go!" Frank shouted and started running up the road toward home.

They slowed down near a house where the sound of a radio floated out over the road. "Do not panic," the announcer was saying. "We repeat. There is no cause for panic. The Japanese attack appears to be over." Kenji and Frank looked at each other and grinned with relief.

"Wait. Someone just brought in a note," the radio voice went on. "It says that a Japanese ship has landed at the north end of the island. If anyone knows more, please call the station. And, remem-ber, keep off the roads so emergency vehicles can get through."

The Glenn Miller Band came on. Frank and Kenji sang along as they walked away. Before they finished the first line, the song stopped. "There *is* no Japanese ship," the radio speaker called out. "Repeat. There is *no* ship. A listener with a good view of the north end called in. I guess all it is safe to say is that rumors are sweeping the island. Just remember, don't panic. We will bring you news as it breaks." And the band was back, playing a love song.

Four army trucks rushed by in a row, stirring up more sand. A blue car hurried after them, then took a turn and squealed down the school's driveway. "Hey, wasn't that Mr. Marsh?" Frank asked.

"Why would the principal go to school Sunday morning?" Kenji wondered aloud.

"Let's go see," Frank said. "It won't take much time. Then we'll go right home." They turned into the driveway.

"Boys, am I ever glad to see you!" called Mr. Marsh. "This school is going to be used for emergency meetings today. We have to tape the windows. That way, if there's another bombing run, the glass won't break into splinters on the people inside." He held out two big rolls of tape. "Here, Frank." *He already knows my name!* Frank thought, happily.

"This is yours, George." Frank looked at Kenji. What would it be like to have two names? Frank was glad he knew Kenji's real name.

"Come on now, boys." Kenji wouldn't take the tape, and Frank didn't want to if Kenji didn't. He knew his mother would be worried. But she'd want him to obey the principal, too. And they'd be doing something to help!

He grabbed both rolls and handed one to Kenji. "I'll race you!" he teased. "Let's start by the front door. I'll go after the windows to the left, you take the right, and we race to the playground door in back."

Kenji shook his head, no.

"*Then* we'll go home, I promise," Frank said. Kenji took the tape.

"Good," Mr. Marsh said. "You can stand on those pineapple crates. I'll tape the second floor windows from inside." He ran and got pails of water for each of them. "Ready? Set? Go!"

Frank grabbed his pineapple crate and set it up beside the building. He knew what to do. He had taped the windows at home in Maryland once when a hurricane was coming. He dipped the tape into water, then stretched up on his toes and stuck the end of the tape to one corner of the glass. Then he unrolled it to the far bottom corner, pressing it into place as he went. Then dip and up again to make a giant X.

By the time he turned the corner of the building, the motions had settled into a pattern. Dip. Up. Down. Dip. Up. Down. Move over to the next window, and dip again. He wondered how far Kenji had gotten. The long side of the building seemed to be going on forever. He tried to remember if there would be two or three windows left when he finally turned the next corner.

When his mind wandered, he saw the men blown off the deck of the *Arizona*. Torpedos churning through the water toward ships tied helplessly at anchor. Flames burning on decks. On piers. On oil slicks. The water itself had seemed on fire. Frank tried to move even faster, to rip the memories out as he ripped the tape off its roll.

At least Kenji had been there to see it with him. It would have been too awful to watch the bombing alone. Kenji was fun to pal around with, Frank thought. At least until he found a real friend. Besides, Kenji wasn't so strange, after all. He was just like anybody else on the baseball team back home. Almost. He began to whistle "Take Me Out to the Ball Game." Finally he rounded the corner and set his crate under the next-to-last window.

"Hey, *haoli,* I'm out of tape," Kenji called from the top of his crate. "Let's see your fastball." He cupped his hands, squatted into a catcher's stance, and almost fell off the crate. Kenji laughed at himself, and Frank hurled the tape squarely into his hands.

"Nice catch," Frank called. It would be great to be on a team with Kenji, he thought.

They were finished in minutes. A block and a half from home, a police car stopped beside them. "You boys," the officer said. "Where are you going?"

"Home," Frank answered.

The officer looked closely at Kenji. "Who are *you?*" he demanded.

"George Imoto, sir," Kenji answered. The policeman kept studying him. "I no live two blocks from here."

"His daddy owns the house where we're staying," Frank put in. The officer wrote both of their names down and told them to hurry home.

When they got to Frank's house, Kenji waved a quick good-bye and kept walking.

"Mom! I'm home!" Frank called as he opened the door. His mother darted out from the kitchen and grabbed him in a long, fierce hug.

"Frank, oh, my Frank," she kept saying. When he could pull away, he saw she'd been crying. "I've been so scared. Your father waited as long as he could for you, but he was needed at the newspaper." She sighed. "They've attacked, Frank. While you were out playing, the Japanese bombed everything."

"Not everything, Mom," Frank said. "Some of the ships are still floating."

"How do you know this?" she asked sharply.

"I saw it." Frank shook his head, trying to keep out the pictures. "Kenji and I watched it all. The bombs and the fires and the torpedos. And, Mom, they hit the *Maryland!*"

"Attention, please." The radio voice burst out from the kitchen. "Private citizens are to prepare their homes for blackout conditions tonight. Stay tuned to this band for further announcements." And as suddenly as it had begun, the radio news was over.

"We have to talk about tonight, Frank," Mrs. Hopkins said. He followed her to the kitchen. "They called for all nurses to report to their nearest hospital to help with wounded soldiers." She handed him a sandwich.

"Are you going?"

"Of course. I have to do something to help!"

Frank smiled. He knew that feeling. "Swell!" he said. While she poured milk for him, he told about helping at the school on the way home. Then he told her about the policeman stopping them and writing down his name.

"Oh, dear." His mother looked out the window. "I wish you had found a safer friend." He knew what she meant. Safe and white. But there were only two other white kids in his class and both of them were girls. All the rest were Japanese, or Chinese, or Korean, or Hawaiian. Why couldn't his mother understand? That was how it *was* in Hawaii!

"Kenji Imoto is just like me, Mom. You should see how he can catch!"

"Well, I hope, so, Franklin. It would fit right in with the plans your father made for you." She gave her white uniform a sharp tug. "While I'm at the hospital, you will be spending the night at the Imotos' with that Kenji."

Chopsticks

Frank looked at the pairs of sandals lined up neatly outside the Imotos' door. "Mom!" he whispered. "Look where they keep their shoes!" There were tiny sandals, large red sandals, and black ones, too. At the end of the row sat a pair of brown men's shoes and a pair of tennis shoes Frank's size. He looked at his own shoes, covered with red dust. "Should I take mine off, too?"

"Oh, dear," Mrs. Hopkins said, "I don't know. No. That wouldn't be good manners." Then she looked at the lines of shoes waiting on both sides of the door and sighed. "Yes, but *hurry*." She pushed the doorbell.

Frank bent to untie his shoelaces. The door opened, and Frank found himself looking at a pair of lady's bare feet. "Welcome," a soft voice said over his head.

"My name is Joyce Hopkins," Frank's mother introduced herself. She grabbed Frank's collar and pulled up on it. "And this is Franklin."

"I'm pleased to meet you, ma'am," Frank said to the feet. He struggled to stand up and put out his hand to shake, but Mrs. Imoto was bowing. Frank stood in amazement, one hand out and one shoe off. No one had ever bowed to him. Should he bow back?

He looked to see what his mother was doing about it. She bowed quickly to Kenji's mother, so Frank did, too. "Will you come in for tea?" Mrs. Imoto's accent made it hard for Frank to understand what she was saying.

"No, thank you," his mother answered. "I have to get to the hospital." Frank could hear the relief in his mother's voice. "But thank you so much for keeping Franklin tonight."

"It is an honor to help you to help our poor boys." Frank looked from Mrs. Imoto to his mother. One was standing in a kimono and bare feet, the other

in a nurse's white uniform and oxford shoes. *Our boys?* "Go then. I will care for Frank-*chan*." *Frank Chan? Hadn't she heard his last name right? How could he tell her without being rude?* Mrs. Imoto was bowing again as Frank's mother left.

"*Mah!* So many dead! So many hurt!" Mrs. Imoto said, and shook her head and sighed. "I will get Kenji-*chan*." *Kenji-chan?* The way she said it sounded nice, whatever it meant. Frank knelt to untie his other shoe.

"*Aloha*." Now Frank was looking at Kenji's stocking feet. "Did you bring your baseball cards?"

Frank pulled the cards from his jacket pocket and grinned. "You bet." He followed Kenji indoors and looked around. The living room was almost empty. No chairs. No rug. One low square table in the middle of the room. "Did you just move in?" he asked.

"No. Grandfather took the house when he came from Japan to cut sugarcane. My father was born here. Me, too."

"Come, put your things in my room," Kenji said. Frank followed him down a hall. Two flags stood in a vase as if they were flowers. One showed the Stars and Stripes. The other had the same rising sun that had glared at Frank from hundreds of bombers just hours ago. He stopped to stare, then had to hurry to follow Kenji into his room.

"Where's the bed? And your desk?" Kenji's bedroom was even worse than the living room. There was nothing but a wide wooden shelf around the wall. "Where do you keep your clothes? Why is everything white?"

Kenji laughed as Frank looked around. "What is wrong with you, *haoli*? You never see a Japanese house?" Frank shook his head. "Give me your jacket." Kenji opened a door that was under the shelf and hung Frank's jacket on a hook inside. Now Frank could see hidden doors all the way around the room.

There was one picture of mountains on the wall. A vase with just three flowers and a twisty leaf in it sat on the shelf. Nothing else.

Kenji opened another door and took his baseball cards off a shelf. "Let's see your Brooklyn Dodgers." He knelt on the floor and began laying his cards out in rows. "Wasn't that some pennant race?"

Frank sat down beside him and pulled out his own Dodgers. He decided to take out the Baltimore Orioles cards, too. Now he felt at home.

"Can you believe that Ted Williams?" Kenji asked. "Batting .406 in his second year in the majors?"

"Yeah. Remember the All-Star Game? Bottom of the ninth, the team down 5–4, Williams hits a homer and drives in two. What a swell play!"

"You know who I'd like to meet?" Kenji asked. Frank shook his head. "Joe DiMaggio."

Frank pulled out his card. "Hits in 56 straight games. That's some record!"

"I bet the whole '41 season goes down in the history books."

"Come. Eat." Mrs. Imoto's voice called them to the living room. The low table in the living room was set with plates and another nearly empty flower vase. No forks. No glasses. And still no chairs.

But there sure were a lot of people, Frank thought. He bowed to Kenji's grandfather and grandmother first. Then to his father. Next, he bowed to an aunt. Finally, he bowed to two younger sisters, Hanako and Emiko. Then it was time to eat.

"Sit here." Kenji patted a cushion on the floor and Frank quickly sat down beside him. Kenji's grandfather was the last in place, settling himself down to the floor slowly and stiffly. Sitting on the floor felt strange to Frank, but it did make the table the right height. Mrs. Imoto opened a big kettle and a spicy smell filled the room. The girls passed out bowls of steaming soup.

Dinner at home with his mom and dad was so quiet and polite. Here dinner was loud and friendly. Nine people talking in three different languages.

Whenever something was said to him in Pidgin or when he spoke in English, it had to be said again in Japanese for the grandparents. It got quiet every time Grandfather spoke, but chatter burst out again whenever he finished. The noise and the warmth swirled around Frank, as strange and delicious as the soup.

After the spoons and bowls were taken away, Mrs. Imoto brought a big bowl of rice and a plate of fish from the kitchen. There were funny-looking vegetables and a dish of pickles, too. It all smelled as good as the soup, but there was nothing to eat it with.

Kenji waved two sticks at him and grinned. "Chopsticks." He pointed to another pair of sticks lying above Frank's plate.

"You eat with sticks?" He watched Kenji grab a bite of fish with the chopsticks, and pop it into his mouth. Frank looked around the table. They were all using sticks. Hanako and Emiko were staring at him as they ate.

"Try," Kenji said.

Frank did try. He dropped his rice on the table. Kenji's sisters giggled and Frank felt his face turn red. He tried again. The rice dropped on his lap. It just wasn't possible. And now all the Imotos were watching him.

Grandfather eased himself up from his place. He took Frank's hand and made him hold the chopsticks in a different way. Grandfather pointed at the fish,

and Frank tried again. This time he got most of it into his mouth.

Hanako and Emiko clapped. Kenji cheered. The table filled with chatter again. "Frank-*chan*," Grandfather said and patted his shoulder.

After dinner, Mr. Imoto began talking to the family in Japanese. Kenji told Frank what he was saying. "There is a blackout tonight. A bomber could use any lights for a target," Kenji explained quietly while his father talked. "No lights can show through the windows. No flashlights. No car lights. Not even cigarettes!" Kenji grinned.

His father's voice got even more serious. "No talking in Japanese out of the house," Kenji repeated for Frank. "No more Japanese flags."

"*Mah!*" Grandfather shouted. The Imoto men argued loudly while all the others looked at their plates.

"What's he saying?" Frank whispered again and again. Kenji just shook his head.

Before it got dark, they pasted tape strips on the windows of the Imoto house. Then the boys walked down to Frank's house and taped those windows, too. Kenji was quiet.

"What were your father and grandfather saying?" Frank tried again.

"We have to be careful," Kenji said.

"We do?"

"Not you. Us." Kenji sounded angry.

"Why?"

"They might attack us, Frank. Or put us in jail. All right?"

"Who? The Japanese?" Frank was confused.

"You, dummy," Kenji muttered and turned to go home. "The *haolis.*"

Air Raid

"Do we *have* to go to bed now?" Emiko was asking her mother when Frank and Kenji came in the door.

"We have no black shades to cover the windows, Emi-*chan*," Mrs. Imoto said. "We must turn out all the lights at dark. You have to be ready."

Frank followed Kenji back to his empty white bedroom. The Japanese flag was gone from the hall. Someone had pinned the American flag out against the wall to look like it was waving in a wind. Or, Frank thought, to cover the empty space beside it.

"So where do we sleep?" Frank finally asked.

Kenji grinned. "On *futons*. Watch." He pulled a straw mat from behind another door and spread it on the floor. Then he took out a thick pad and a blanket and put them on top of the mat. Frank made a bed for himself the same way. He looked at it for a moment, then slid it across the floor to be nearer to Kenji. They could talk in a blackout, even if they couldn't keep the lights on. "How can you sleep on the floor?" he had to ask.

"How you sleep on a bed?" Kenji's answer was no answer at all. "Beds are too soft," he explained. "They bounce. You can fall out, get hurt. I no can sleep on bed."

It still sounded strange, Frank thought, looking down at his *futon*. "What about pillows?" he asked.

Kenji grabbed two small sacks from the top shelf and tossed them onto the *futons*. "But those are beanbags!" Frank gasped.

Kenji shrugged and lay down on the bed he'd made for himself on the floor. A faint glow from the sunset came through the window shades. In the dim light, Frank watched Kenji settle his head on the beanbag.

He looked around the room. *There is no way I can sleep here*, Frank thought. *The house is full of strangers. And strange things.*

"Come on, *haoli*," Kenji said at last. "Try it." The

way he said *haoli* made Frank smile. Kenji gave the word the same warm sound that Frank's teammates had back in Maryland when they talked to him.

Frank tried to make his head comfortable on the beanbag. The beans inside shifted and rattled loudly in his ear, so he stopped squirming.

"Kenji?" he asked into the darkness. "What does it mean when your mother calls me 'Frank-*chan*'?"

"It means she likes you. *O-yasumi nasai, haoli.*"

"What!?"

"*O-yasumi nasai* means good night."

"*O-yasumi nasai,* Kenji."

A screaming siren made Frank jump from his sleep. Where was he? What was the siren? Where was his mother? Everything was wrong.

He tried to get out of bed, but the floor was right there where air should be. The window was on the wrong side.

The door opened. The light of a small candle lit Mrs. Imoto's face. Frank relaxed. That explained where he was. But what was all the noise?

The siren wailed on and on. Mrs. Imoto came close and bent down between the two boys. "It is an air raid," she said loudly. Frank could barely hear her. "I do not think there are planes in attack. I have radio on. I will let you know." And she was gone.

And, suddenly, the siren was gone, too. The silence was huge. Frank listened hard for any sound. Had he lost his hearing?

"Just a test," Mrs. Imoto called from the hallway. "No danger. *O-yasumi nasai.*" And Frank could hear her footsteps padding away down the hall.

"Kenji? Can you get back to sleep?"

"No. You?"

"No chance," Frank said. "You want to go outside and look at the blackout?"

There was a long silence. They shouldn't go out. Frank knew it. They could get into a lot of trouble. Kenji would say no, and that would end the whole crazy idea.

"Yes."

"What!" Frank said.

"You no can hear? Let's go."

They slipped through the back door and out into a moonless night.

Stars were everywhere across the sky. Their faint, blue light fell on the houses, the trees, the roads, and the bushes. Frank took a deep breath. The air was full of the strong sweet smell of night flowers. Tree frogs called from every bush.

"Come on!" Frank whispered. He wanted to see his own home in this spooky light. Frank led the way to the road.

"Halt!" A man's voice barked from behind them.

Both boys ran. They fled straight down the sidewalk, away from the voice, but not away from the footsteps. The man was running, too, and his legs were longer. They could hear him catch up.

"Stop, you stupid kids," he panted from right behind them. They did. They couldn't get away. Frank turned to stand beside Kenji. Standing outdoors, barefoot and in his pajamas, Frank felt almost naked.

The starlight glittered on—a gun? He started running again, but the man grabbed his arm.

"What do you clowns think this is?" the man asked angrily. "A *game?* We're at war! I'm supposed to shoot anybody who doesn't stop when I call 'halt.' " He shook Frank's arm. "I could have shot you."

"And *you.*" He looked at Kenji's face. "You stay indoors. The way people are feeling tonight, you might be shot as a spy whether you stopped or not."

"Now, let's walk on home." The man headed back up the sidewalk. Frank and Kenji dragged on behind him. The adventure was over.

Frank looked at the gun on the man's shoulder. He was keeping his hand against it as they walked. Frank wondered if that was to keep it quiet. Or to keep it ready. "You going to tell our folks?" he whispered.

"Naw. I got a boy like you. He'd want to be out

tonight, too," the man said. Then he growled, "But he better not be!"

"Halt!" another voice called from up the street. "Who goes there?"

"It's me, Will. All clear."

Frank and Kenji followed silently to the Imoto house. "I live here, sir," Kenji whispered.

"Then *stay* there!" He ruffled Kenji's hair before he strode on into the darkness.

Frank got back into bed, and watched as slivers of dawn slowly began to glow around the window shade. The Imoto house was very strange, he thought, but it was peaceful. Quiet. Safe. It was nice to think that no matter what happened with the war, here he would be Frank-*chan*.

Kenji was already sleeping, his head resting on the beanbag. Frank had one more question to ask, but it could wait. First thing in the morning he would ask Kenji how to say "friend" in Japanese. Frank smiled and fell asleep.

The bombing of Pearl Harbor happened just as I described it. The Japanese planned their surprise attack for early Sunday morning, December 7, 1941. They knew many servicemen would be away from their posts and the Hawaiians would just be getting out of bed.

In less than two hours of bombing, 2,300 Americans died, 960 were lost, and 1,100 more were wounded. Eight battleships lay sunk in Pearl Harbor, along with three cruisers, three destroyers, and three other ships. Japan was trying to destroy America's power in the Pacific so they could take over. Their plan didn't work.

The Japanese did not bomb Pearl Harbor's huge oil tanks, their ammunition storage buildings, or the U.S. submarines. They missed three aircraft carriers which were out at sea. They did not ruin the ship repair docks. Within six months, our Pacific fleet was stronger than it had ever been—and it went on to win the war that started in Pearl Harbor.

I made up Frank and Kenji and their story at Pearl

Harbor. To make it realistic, I looked in old guide-books and talked to people who'd been in Hawaii 50 years ago. Then I spoke with my son Hal's karate teacher, a Japanese-American named Harry Tadao Imoto.

It was as if I had met the real-life Kenji. Not only had Tadao lived in Hawaii as a child, but he actually watched the bombing of Pearl Harbor (though he stood on top of a pigeon coop, not a tree fort). He remembered how some of the island children used to tease *haolis*. He said that he used to feel sorry for the newcomers, and tried to make friends with them instead.

The true story took a cruel turn after the bombing. Thousands of Japanese-Americans were arrested as spies. Whole families were taken from their homes on the mainland. They were sent to live in vast prisons called internment camps. In Hawaii it was different.

Hawaiians are a mix of native islanders, Caucasians, Asian-Americans, and other groups. All of them work together to run the shops and farms, the schools and towns of the islands. Japanese-Americans were not the enemy in World War II. The islanders knew that from working side by side with them. There were a few arrests, but there were no internment camps in Hawaii.

K.V.K.